SHADOW

ELLEN MILES

SCHOLASTIC INC.
New York London Toronto Auckland
Sydney Mexico City Hong Kong New Delhi

For Katie

ISBN-13: 978-0-439-79381-0
ISBN-10: 0-439-79381-5

35 34 19 20 21 22 23/0

Printed in the U.S.A. 40

First printing, January 2006

CHAPTER ONE

"Charles, why did you move the forks?" Lizzie felt around on the table until her hand touched a pile of silverware. She could tell by the smooth shape that she was feeling spoons. Where were the forks?

"I didn't move anything," Charles called from the living room. "I'm not even near the table."

Lizzie felt around again. "Ah, there they are!" She picked up the handful of forks and began moving carefully around the table, setting one down at each place.

"Told you," Charles said. "What are you doing, anyway?"

Lizzie could hear her younger brother walking into the dining room. "I'm pretending to be blind,"

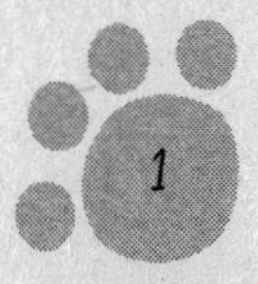

she told him. She had tied a silky blue scarf over her eyes. It made a good blindfold.

"Um, okay," Charles said. "Why?"

"I want to know what it's like," Lizzie explained. "Our class is reading a book called *The Story of My Life,* by Helen Keller. Did you ever hear of her?"

Charles shook his head.

"Well, did you?" Lizzie asked when she didn't hear him answer.

"Oh —" said Charles when he remembered that Lizzie couldn't see him shaking his head. "No."

"I guess you will when you're in fourth grade," Lizzie said. She always liked to remind Charles that she was older and wiser. Knowing his sister couldn't see him, Charles made a face and stuck out his tongue.

"Anyway," Lizzie went on, "she was this girl who was blind and deaf. She couldn't talk, either. Can you imagine?"

This time, Charles remembered to say no as he shook his head.

"Well, I'm trying to," Lizzie said. "I mean, I'm at least trying to imagine what it would be like to be blind."

"Did Helen Keller have a Seeing Eye dog?" Charles asked.

"Good question," Lizzie said. "No, she loved dogs and had lots of them, but no guide dogs. They didn't really have guide dogs for blind people when she was growing up." Lizzie heard Charles sigh. She knew he was probably rolling his eyes because she sounded like a book again. Lizzie couldn't help it. She liked facts. Especially facts about dogs.

Lizzie and Charles were both crazy about dogs. So was the Bean, their little brother. In fact, the Bean — whose real name was Adam — liked to pretend that he *was* a dog. He liked to play with dog toys and sleep on a dog bed, and he barked more often than he talked.

But even though the Bean acted like a dog, he was not a dog. So Lizzie and Charles still begged

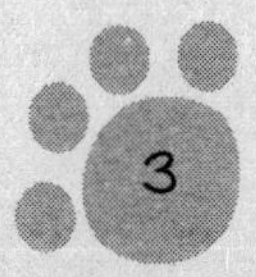

their parents for a dog almost every day. Mr. Peterson, their father, loved dogs, too. But he and Mrs. Peterson — who had always been a "cat person" — agreed that the family was not ready for a full-time dog. As Mom always said, dogs were a big commitment. That meant they were a lot of work and responsibility.

Lizzie knew that. And she was ready. Ready to walk a dog every day, feed it, groom it, and train it. She had proved it, too. The Petersons had been the foster family for two puppies recently, taking care of them for a little while until they found them forever families. Charles and Lizzie had worked really hard to take good care of the puppies. With help from their parents, they had started to train the puppies, too.

"How's Snowball?" Lizzie asked Charles, thinking of their most recent foster puppy. The little west highland white terrier now lived with Mrs. Peabody, who was Charles's Grandbuddy. Grandbuddies was a school program where kids

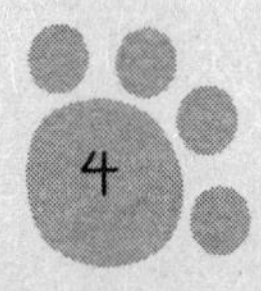

visited with older folks who lived at apartments called The Meadows.

"He's great!" Charles reported. "Mrs. Peabody taught him how to put his own toys away. He carries them over to a basket in the corner. Then he comes and waits for a treat."

"Snowball's such a little smartie," Lizzie said. She felt for the stack of plates and began to go around the table again, putting a plate at each setting. "I think he might be even smarter than Goldie." Goldie was a golden retriever puppy the Petersons had fostered. She lived next door with Charles's best friend, Sammy, and his family, and their older golden retriever, Rufus.

"I don't know about that," Charles said. "Goldie's pretty smart. She already learned how to open the cabinet where Sammy's mom keeps the dog food."

"That's just because she's hungry," Lizzie said, laughing. "Golden retrievers are big chowhounds. They love food more than anything. But Goldie's no dummy, that's for sure."

"You can say that again," said Mr. Peterson, coming into the room from the kitchen.

"Goldie's no dummy," Lizzie repeated with a straight face, "that's for sure." Then she cracked up.

Mr. Peterson laughed, too. "Why the blindfold?" he asked.

Lizzie explained again about Helen Keller.

"Hmm," said Mr. Peterson. "Interesting. Well, you did a very nice job setting the table, even without being able to see. But you're going to have to squeeze in one more place. We're having company for dessert tonight."

"Who?" Charles and Lizzie asked together.

"Dr. Gibson," their dad told them. "Remember, the veterinarian we took Snowball to? Your mom and I invited her over. She called today and said she has something to talk to us about." He smiled at them. "And I have a feeling it might have to do with a puppy."

CHAPTER TWO

"A puppy?" Lizzie pulled off her blindfold. Suddenly, she was too excited to concentrate on pretending to be blind. "What *about* a puppy?"

Dad shrugged and held up both hands. "I have no idea," he said. "Your mom spoke to her." Then he checked his watch. "By the way, Mom and the Bean will be home any minute, so let's get dinner on the table. I made macaroni and cheese."

"But Dad!" Charles said. "Are we getting another puppy to foster, or what?"

Lizzie sighed. Sometimes Charles just didn't listen. "Dad doesn't *know*," she said. "Come on, help me finish setting the table."

They all rushed around for a few minutes, and

by the time Mom and the Bean walked in, dinner was all ready.

"We heard about the puppy!" Lizzie said, as her mom took off her coat and put a bag of groceries down on the counter.

"Oh?" asked her mom, raising her eyebrows. "What exactly did you hear?"

"Well," Lizzie admitted, "not much, really. Just that Dr. Gibson is coming over later and it might be about a puppy."

Mom nodded. "Well, that's about all I know, too," she said. "I was rushing around when Dr. Gibson called and I really didn't have time to talk. But we'll find out more soon, I'm sure."

"We're getting another puppy, we're getting another puppy," chanted Charles, hopping around the room.

"Uppy! Uppy!" yelled the Bean. He knew that word. He *loved* that word.

"I wonder what kind," Lizzie said. "I hope it's a big dog this time. Great Dane? Poodle? Saint

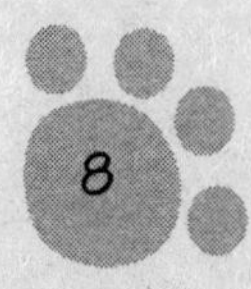

Bernard? Even an Airedale would be cool." Lizzie loved looking at her "Dog Breeds of the World" poster and learning about all the different kinds of dogs there were. She loved big dogs best — in fact, she didn't even really think little dogs counted. "Really," she finished, "any puppy would be great. Look at Snowball. He was a little dog, and he was adorable and smart and so, so much fun." Lizzie knew she was rattling on a little but she couldn't help herself. She was excited.

"Whoa, whoa," said Mom. "Hold on there, kids. Let's wait and find out what Dr. Gibson has to tell us."

Lizzie loved her dad's macaroni and cheese, but that night she hardly tasted it as she wolfed it down.

Charles didn't even bother arguing about how many bites of broccoli he had to eat. He just finished what was on his plate without even seeming to notice.

The Bean crawled around on the floor by their

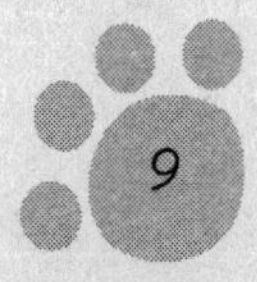

feet, the way he always did at mealtimes, pretending to be a dog. Every so often he would come over to Lizzie's chair and put his chin on her knee, asking to be patted. "Good dog," she said as she stroked his hair. The Bean liked that.

"Nice job on your broccoli, Charles," Mom said. "You ate it all."

That reminded Charles of a joke. *Everything* reminded Charles of a joke. "Hey, why was six afraid of seven?" he asked.

"Why?" Dad asked. He always humored Charles.

"Because seven eight nine," Charles said. "Get it? Seven ate nine!"

He cracked up.

Lizzie rolled her eyes. She'd heard that one a million times. "That joke is so old, the last time I heard it I fell off my dinosaur," she said.

Charles stuck his tongue out at her.

"Well, I thought it was funny," Dad said. "Seven eight nine. I'll have to remember to tell that one down at the firehouse."

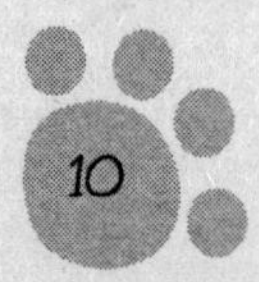

Mr. Peterson was a fireman, and Mrs. Peterson was a reporter for the local newspaper. Sometimes Mom wrote articles about big fires that Dad helped put out.

"I think it's your turn to clear the table, Charles," Mom said when they were done eating.

"I'll help," Lizzie said, jumping up. "He helped me set it."

Mom smiled. Lizzie knew how much Mom loved it when they helped out without being asked. She figured this was a good time to get on Mom's good side, if there might be a puppy in the picture.

Lizzie was loading the dishwasher when the doorbell rang. "I'll get it!" she yelled as she dashed past Charles. She threw the door open.

"Hello," said Dr. Gibson.

"Oh!" said Lizzie, taking a deep breath. Cuddled in the vet's arms was the cutest puppy she had ever seen. His coat was a shiny, silky black, and the pup looked back at Lizzie with intelligent, sparkling brown eyes. His forehead was wrinkled

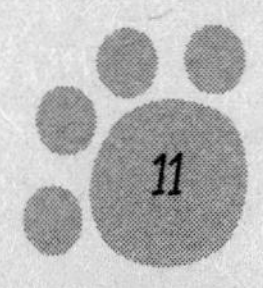

in the cutest way, as if he were worried about something. He was a serious little pup.

The puppy liked the girl right away. He liked everybody, *but especially people who smiled at him that way. Would she like him, too? As soon as he had a chance, he was going to lick her face all over.*

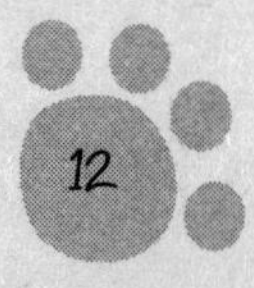

CHAPTER THREE

"This is Shadow," said Dr. Gibson. She didn't seem to notice that Lizzie didn't say hello or invite her in. "I know I shouldn't have brought him over without asking first, but I just couldn't stand to leave him home alone."

By then the rest of the family had crowded in behind Lizzie.

"Wow," said Charles. "He's so cute! How old is he?"

"Aww," said Dad. "What a great little pup."

"Uppy!" yelled the Bean, reaching up to try to pat the puppy.

Even Mom, the cat lover, was impressed. "Would you look at him?" she asked. "Isn't he something?"

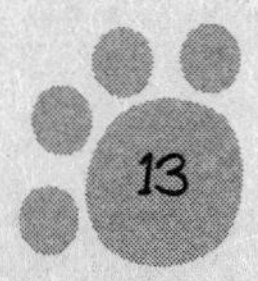

Then she seemed to remember her manners. "Come in, why don't you, Dr. Gibson?"

"Call me Katie, please," said the doctor as she came inside. She smiled at Lizzie. "You look as if you're itching to hold this puppy. Want to take him while I get my coat off?"

Lizzie held out her arms, and the vet handed the puppy to her. His soft, warm weight made Lizzie sigh happily. And when he put one paw on either side of her neck in a sort of puppy hug, she felt as if her heart would burst. "Hello, Shadow," she whispered into one of his silky ears. "Good boy." The puppy nuzzled her cheek with his nose, then licked her face all over, which made her giggle.

Then the puppy struggled to get down, and Lizzie carefully lowered him to the floor. He ran straight for the Bean, who was laughing and clapping his hands.

"Grab him!" said Mrs. Peterson.

Lizzie wasn't sure whether her mom meant

Shadow or the Bean, but there wasn't time, anyway.

"It's okay," said Dr. Gibson. "Shadow is terrific with little kids. He played with my one-year-old nephew all day today. He's just a puppy, but he acts almost like a grown-up dog."

They all watched as the Bean threw his arms around Shadow. "Uppy!" the Bean cried. Shadow's frown disappeared. His little tail wagged so fast that it was nothing but a black blur. The pudgy puppy licked the Bean's cheeks, nose, and ears.

This little person was so much fun! It was just like being back with his brothers and sisters, who loved to tumble all over one another and wrestle and play. Right away, Shadow knew he would do anything for this little person. Anything!

"Shadow's a pretty special pup," Dr. Gibson told them when they were all sitting down to eat the chocolate cake Mom had brought home. By then,

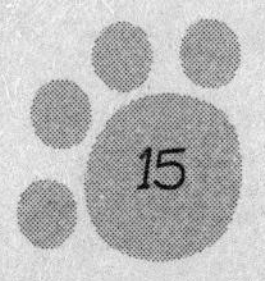

Lizzie had scooped up Shadow again and he was sitting in her lap while she ate. The Bean stood next to Lizzie's chair, stroking Shadow's ears. "He's a purebred Labrador retriever, with papers and everything," the vet explained.

"Papers, like to pee on?" Charles sounded confused.

Lizzie smiled. "No," she told him. "That's for housebreaking. The kind of papers she's talking about are proof that he is a purebred dog. They tell who his mother and father are, and where he comes from."

"That's right, Lizzie," said the vet, sounding impressed. "Anyway, this special pup needs a home. A family in town bought him from a breeder, but almost right away they found out that their son is allergic to dogs! So they asked me to find him a good home, and I thought of you."

She smiled at Charles and Lizzie. "You did such a good job taking care of Snowball and finding him a home. Mrs. Peabody brought him in the

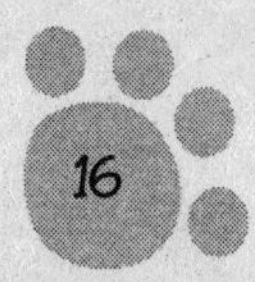

other day for a checkup, and he looked so healthy and happy. Remember how sick he was when we first saw him?"

Lizzie nodded. But she wasn't thinking about Snowball. She was thinking about Shadow, the adorable little puppy who was now nestled in her arms, fast asleep. "Can we, Mom?" she asked. "Can we keep Shadow?"

"Keep?" Mom asked. "Or foster?"

Lizzie already knew she would love to keep Shadow forever. But Mom probably wouldn't say yes to that. "Foster," she said. "Just until we find him a really great home."

"Yeah, foster!" Charles agreed quickly. Lizzie knew Charles was like her. He would do anything to keep the puppy — even if only for a little while.

Mom nodded thoughtfully. "It's hard to say no to this little guy," she said. "What do you say, Paul?"

"I'm all for it, if you are," Dad said.

"One thing I should say," said Dr. Gibson, "is that it would be best if you can find Shadow a

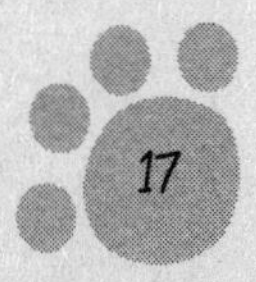

permanent home quickly. He is only nine weeks old, and this is an important time for him to learn how to be part of a family. We don't want him to get too attached to you and then have to start all over again."

Mrs. Peterson was nodding. Lizzie and Charles just looked at each other, and Lizzie knew they were thinking the very same thing. Maybe *they* could be Shadow's permanent home.

But then Mom spoke up. "That makes sense," she said. "And the timing works for us, too. We have a family vacation planned in a couple of weeks. We're visiting relatives in South Carolina over spring break."

Lizzie knew that her mother was right. She was really looking forward to seeing her cousins. They had two really cool dogs, named Pogo and Winnie, to play with.

Lizzie, Charles, and the Bean always had the best time in South Carolina. And it was true that it wouldn't be fair to leave a puppy as young as

Shadow in a kennel for almost two weeks. But Lizzie knew it was also true that giving up Shadow would be one of the hardest things she'd ever have to do. She was already in love with the little black puppy with the serious face.

Shadow felt warm and safe on the girl's lap. He knew she would take good care of him. And he would take care of her, too. He squirmed into a more comfortable position, sighed happily, and went back to sleep.

CHAPTER FOUR

By the end of the weekend, the whole family was in love with Shadow, and he loved them all, too. The puppy and the Bean seemed to have an extra-special bond. They were never apart. They roamed all over the house together. Sometimes the Bean was toddling and the puppy was scampering after him. Sometimes Shadow was trotting ahead and the Bean was trying to keep up. They napped together curled up on a soft, fleecy dog bed and took turns playing with the Bean's favorite stuffed toys. Shadow seemed to think it was his job to protect and watch over the Bean, as if the Bean were a younger puppy who needed his care.

Shadow was a good puppy. He was already

mostly housebroken, and he usually whimpered at the door if he needed to go out.

And he loved to cuddle. Lizzie spent most of Sunday evening with Shadow sleeping on her lap while she watched a movie. She loved the little puppy noises he made in his sleep while she stroked his silky ears. Once in a while he would wake partway up, stretch and yawn, and kiss her on the chin. That was the best.

Lizzie and Charles had a hard time leaving the house on Monday morning when it was time to head for school. "Good-bye, Shadow," Lizzie said, scooping him up for one more hug. She kissed the top of his silky head. "You be a good boy, okay?" She put him down and he bounded back to the Bean's side.

Shadow was sorry to see the girl and boy leave, but now he could concentrate on the smallest person in the house. He loved his new friend so much!

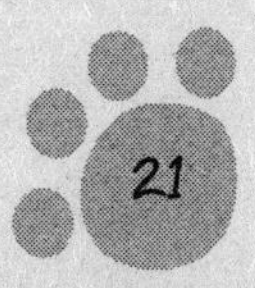

Charles and his best friend, Sammy, chattered about the new puppy all the way to school. Lizzie walked behind them, wishing she had a best friend, too. It would be fun to tell somebody about all the funny things that Shadow had done over the weekend, like sticking his head into the Bean's toy chest and pulling out a stuffed bear that was twice as big as he was.

Charles was lucky. When the Petersons had moved to Littleton last summer, Charles had found a best friend who lived right next door. But there were no girls Lizzie's age in the neighborhood. She was friendly with most of the girls in her class, but she didn't have a *best* friend.

Often at recess Lizzie spent her time reading or looking things up on the computer instead of playing jump rope or kickball. Lizzie didn't really mind that, but once in a while she thought it would be nice to have someone to share her secrets or exciting news with.

She thought about telling the whole class about

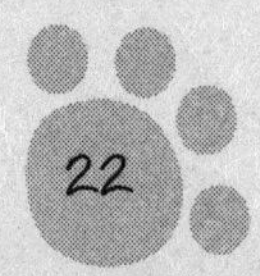

Shadow during their morning meeting, but at the last minute she decided not to. Somehow she wanted to keep him to herself for a little while. Knowing she was going to have to find him a good home and give him up soon made him seem even more precious to her.

Anyway, that day everybody was talking about Helen Keller. Mrs. Abeson had asked how many of them had been reading the book over the weekend, and lots of hands went up. "What interesting things did you find out about Helen Keller?" Mrs. Abeson asked.

"I don't see how Helen Keller could climb trees and stuff like that," Noah said. "I mean, she couldn't *see* anything."

"Blind people can do lots of things," said a girl named Maria Santiago, who was even newer to Littleton Elementary than Lizzie. Usually Maria was really shy. Lizzie was a little surprised to hear her speak up.

"That's right," Lizzie said. "I found that out this

weekend. I spent a lot of time wearing a blindfold so I could see what it was like to be blind. It wasn't so hard to learn my way around the house." Lizzie didn't mention how many times she had almost tripped over toys that Shadow and the Bean had left lying all over the place. "The only thing was, I didn't feel *really* blind because I could still see light and dark through the blindfold."

Again, Maria put up her hand. "Lots of blind people see light and shadow," she said softly. "The world isn't completely dark for most of them."

Lizzie looked at her. All of a sudden, Maria was starting to seem like a little bit of a know-it-all. What had happened to the girl who hardly ever spoke in class unless she was called on? Lizzie shrugged. "Maybe," she said. "Another thing I noticed was that my hearing didn't really get any better. Supposedly when you're blind your other senses — like hearing and touch — start to make up for it, but maybe that takes a while to happen."

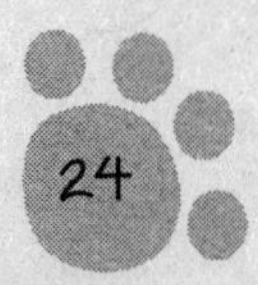

Maria was shaking her head. Mrs. Abeson called on her. “Maria? Did you have something to say?”

“Well, only that it’s kind of a myth that blind people can hear better,” said Maria. “Their hearing is the same. They just learn to pay more attention to what they hear.”

Mrs. Abeson nodded. “That makes sense,” she said.

Lizzie frowned. Wasn’t that the same thing *she* had just said? And how did Maria know all this stuff, anyway? Lizzie couldn’t help being curious. But Mrs. Abeson had moved on to asking everyone to get their math homework out, so there was no chance to find out more.

The rest of the day dragged by. Lizzie couldn’t wait to get home and see Shadow again. When the last bell rang, she grabbed her jacket and met Charles and Sammy outside. The three of them ran almost all the way home.

CHAPTER FIVE

"Shadow!" Lizzie called when she and Charles got home. "Here, pup!" She was dying to see the little black puppy. Where was he?

"We're up here!" Mom called from upstairs. "I'm just putting away some laundry. Be right down."

Charles and Sammy headed into the kitchen to find a snack. Sammy was always eating at the Petersons'. Lizzie knew he would head straight to the cookie jar and help himself.

Lizzie walked into the front hallway and looked up the stairs just in time to see the Bean running toward the landing on the second floor. He was laughing his googly laugh and waving his hands

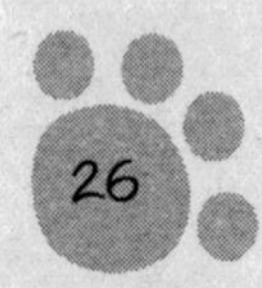

in the air — and he wasn't watching where he was going.

Until a few months ago, the Petersons had always closed off the top of the stairs with a baby gate so that the Bean wouldn't fall downstairs. But lately they had not used the gate as much. The Bean was getting bigger, and he knew about being careful near the stairs.

Usually.

But not this time. He was playing "chase me" with Shadow, and he was running as fast as his little legs could go.

"Watch out!" Lizzie yelled. "Adam!" She hardly ever used his real name, but it popped right out of her mouth. She started to run up the stairs, hoping she could catch her little brother if he started to tumble.

Just then, Shadow put on a burst of speed and ran toward the Bean, coming between the toddling boy and the top of the stairs.

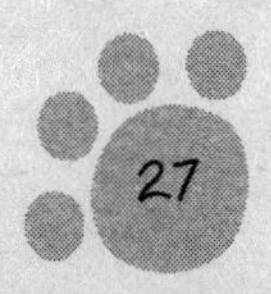

Oh, no! Shadow could tell the little person was in danger! But he knew he could help his friend. He would push him away from the stairs so he wouldn't fall! Faster, faster!

The puppy bumped into the Bean, shoving him back onto the landing.

The Bean sat back with a surprised look on his face. Lizzie wondered if he was going to burst into tears. Then, after a moment, he started laughing again.

Lizzie charged the rest of the way up the stairs, knelt down next to the Bean, and put an arm around him. "Are you okay, buddy?" she asked, even though she could see that he was. "Good dog, Shadow," she said, putting her other arm around the pup. "You saved him!"

"What happened?" Mom asked, coming out of Charles's room.

"Mom, Shadow was amazing! He kept the Bean from falling down the stairs," Lizzie reported. She

scooped the pup into her arms and gave him a big kiss on the head. He gave her that serious look of his before he kissed her back.

Shadow didn't know what all the fuss was about, but he liked it. Kisses and hugs were always good. But so was running around! Running around was really *good.*

Shadow squirmed to get down. "Uppy!" yelled the Bean, jumping to his feet for another game of "chase me."

Mom sighed. "Good for Shadow. But I guess we'd better get that gate back up for a while," she said. "These two have been running wild all day. You would think they would tire themselves out, but no. They just tire *me* out." She smiled at her son and the puppy, but then gave Lizzie a serious look. "As much as the Bean loves Shadow, we really do have to find him a home. And soon."

Lizzie nodded. "Okay," she said. "But it has to be the *right* home. Shadow can't go to just any old family. He's a special dog."

By then, Charles and Sammy had joined them. They were each munching on an apple. "Hi, Shadow," Charles said, giving the puppy a hug. "You *are* a special dog."

"I know how we can find him a home," Sammy volunteered when he, Lizzie, and Charles were sitting in Lizzie's room a little later. They had offered to watch Shadow and the Bean for a while so Mrs. Peterson could work on an article she was writing. "We can take him to the rummage sale at the recreation center this weekend."

"What, sell him for fifty cents?" Lizzie asked. "I don't think so. This dog came from a good breeder. He has papers. That means he's worth hundreds of dollars."

"But we're not going to sell him for hundreds of dollars, either, are we?" Charles asked.

Lizzie shook her head. "No. We'll give him away. But it has to be the right family." She pulled out a piece of paper and started to make a list. "They should have a big house," she began, "because he needs lots of room to run around."

"Or at least a big yard," said Charles.

"Good!" said Lizzie. "With a fence around it, so he'll be safe."

"I think the family should like to do stuff outdoors," Sammy said. "Because Shadow is going to be an outdoorsy kind of dog. He wouldn't want to be cooped up inside all the time."

Lizzie made some more notes. She looked over at the Bean and Shadow, who were finally napping on her bed. Shadow was snuggled right up next to the Bean. He was snoring a little, just tiny puppy snores. "I think Shadow should go to a home where there's a little kid like the Bean," she said softly. She wrote that down. Then she read the list out loud.

"The perfect home sounds just like *our* home," Charles said. "Why can't *we* keep Shadow?"

"I wish we could," Lizzie said. She really, really did. "But I guess the timing just isn't right, especially with our vacation and all. At least we get to keep him for a while. That's the cool thing about fostering puppies. We get to spend time with all kinds of different dogs."

CHAPTER SIX

The next day, Lizzie decided it was time to tell everyone in her class about Shadow. First of all, he was such an amazing puppy that she just had to boast about him. And second of all, he really did need a home. Maybe it would help to spread the word if she told people at school.

When the Petersons were trying to find a home for Goldie, they had put up signs. Lizzie was planning to make a sign about Shadow as soon as she had time.

The minute the morning meeting began, Lizzie raised her hand. When Mrs. Abeson called on her, she started telling all about how her family was fostering Shadow and about how cute and funny

and smart he was. "He even kept my little brother from falling down the stairs!" she reported.

Maria gave her an admiring glance. "He sounds like a great puppy," she said. "I wish my family could take him, but we already have a dog. His name is Simba, and he —"

"I forgot to say that Shadow already knows how to come when you call his name!" Lizzie interrupted. She didn't mean to be rude. She was just excited about Shadow. When she saw Maria's face fall, she felt bad. But it really was still her turn to talk. "Anyway, if anybody hears of a really nice family that's looking for a dog, let me know," Lizzie finished.

"We'll be sure to do that," said Mrs. Abeson. "A wonderful puppy like that deserves a special home."

After that, Noah had to tell about how his guinea pig was going to have babies, and Daniel said that his pet snake was shedding its skin, and Caroline said that her cat, Flower, liked to catch

mice and leave them in her dad's slippers. It was like pet day at morning meeting.

"We're going to meet a very special pet tomorrow, as part of our unit on Helen Keller," Mrs. Abeson said. Her eyes were sparkling. "But it's a surprise." Lizzie saw her glance over at Maria. Maria blushed. What was *that* about?

Before she could ask any questions, Mrs. Abeson said it was time for math. As they headed for their desks, Lizzie touched Maria on the shoulder. "Is it your pet that's coming?" she asked.

"It's a surprise," Maria whispered.

Lizzie made a face. Maria was probably just still mad because Lizzie interrupted her. Oh, well. She could keep her dumb secret.

Once again, the school day dragged by. All Lizzie wanted to do was spend time with Shadow before she had to give him up. When the day was over, she raced out of school, hardly waiting for Sammy and Charles.

"Where's Shadow?" she demanded when she found her dad in the kitchen.

"Probably upstairs with your mom and the Bean," Dad said. "Want me to make you some ants on a log for a snack?"

Ants on a log was one of Lizzie and Charles's favorite snacks. It was celery sticks with peanut butter spread on them, and raisins sprinkled onto the peanut butter. The raisins were supposed to look like ants on a log. Really they just looked like raisins on peanut butter. But still, Lizzie loved the snack. "Sure," she said. "But first I have to find Shadow."

She ran upstairs. "Mom!" she said when she found her mom working at her computer. "Where's Shadow?"

"Downstairs with your dad, I think," her mom said, staring at the screen.

Lizzie shook her head. "Not there," she said. "Where's the Bean?"

“Napping,” her mom said. “He and Shadow played hard this afternoon.”

Lizzie went down the hall to the Bean’s room. Shadow was probably sleeping right next to the Bean on the Bean’s new “big-boy bed.”

But the puppy wasn’t there — and neither was the Bean.

Lizzie ran back to her mom. “Mom, the Bean’s not in his bed! He and Shadow are *both* lost.”

“What?” said Mom. She jumped up and ran to the Bean’s room.

Lizzie ran downstairs to get Charles and Dad. “Shadow and the Bean are both missing!” she told them.

Dad was just handing Charles a glass of milk. He stared at Lizzie. “Missing?” he asked. “How could that be? Your mom and I have been home all afternoon.”

“We’ll find them,” said Charles. “They have to be somewhere in the house.”

They started by looking in all the bedrooms.

No sign of Shadow or the Bean.

Then they checked the living room, the dining room, and the den.

"Shadow! Adam!" Lizzie was calling their names all over the house. This was terrible! Where was her little brother? And what about Shadow? The Petersons were responsible for the puppy. They were his foster family. They were supposed to keep him safe until they found him a forever home. That was their whole job! If they messed up, who would ever give them another puppy to foster?

CHAPTER SEVEN

Then Lizzie heard it: A tiny, distant bark. And a whimper.

Shadow didn't like this place. It was dark and lonely. He had come in to keep the little boy safe, but then the door had slammed shut and they were both stuck inside.

"Shadow!" she cried. "Did you hear that, Charles?"

Charles nodded. "I think it came from the Bean's room," he said, looking confused.

They all ran back upstairs and into the Bean's room. "Shadow?" Lizzie called.

Another bark. It was coming from the closet!

Dad yanked open the door, and Mom swooped in to pick up the Bean. "Oh, honey," she said, hugging him.

Shadow bounced out, looking as happy as always. Lizzie bent down to pick him up and give him a kiss. She was so relieved to see him — and the Bean, of course!

Yay! Shadow was glad they had finally heard him. Maybe it was time for a treat! He had certainly earned one.

"Ball!" said the Bean, pointing back toward the closet.

Dad shook his head. "He must have woken up from his nap and gone in there to get his ball," he said. "Shadow followed him, the door closed, and then they were both trapped."

"Good thing the Bean had his guardian angel with him!" Mom said, hugging the Bean again. "I'm glad you're both okay."

* * *

The next morning at school, Lizzie still felt horrible about what had happened. How long had Bean and Shadow been trapped? Fostering puppies was a serious job!

But then something happened that made her forget everything else.

"Remember I mentioned yesterday that we were going to meet a very special pet?" said Mrs. Abeson, right after math. "Well, our guest is here. Maria, would you introduce him?"

Blushing, Maria got up, went to the door, and opened it. "This is Simba," she said as a big, stocky, yellow Labrador retriever walked into the room.

The dog was wearing a harness with a leather handle. Holding the harness was a woman who looked like a grown-up version of Maria.

"And this is my mom," Maria added. "She's blind."

For a second, the classroom was completely quiet. Then it exploded into noise as everyone started asking questions at once.

“How old is he?”

“Can we pat him?”

“How does he know which way to go?”

Lizzie was probably the only one in class who wasn’t shouting out questions. She just sat there, staring at Simba and at Maria’s mother. Lizzie felt her face flush red as she remembered how she had acted the day before, showing off how much she knew about blind people. Of course Maria knew more than she did! When Maria went back to her seat, Lizzie gave her a special smile, hoping she would understand how sorry she felt. Maria smiled back.

Mrs. Abeson called for everyone to quiet down. “One question at a time,” she said. She asked Maria’s mom if she’d like to sit down, and told her how to find the chair she had set up at the front of the classroom. When Mrs. Santiago was sitting, with Simba lying quietly next to her, Mrs. Abeson called on Noah.

“Where did you get Simba?” asked Noah.

"I got him from a foundation that trains guide dogs for the blind," said Mrs. Santiago. "He spent the first year of his life with puppy-raisers. Those are families who volunteer to bring up future guide dogs and teach them basic manners. Then the foundation trained him to work with a blind person. Then they trained *me* how to work with a dog!" She smiled. "Finally, Simba and I were matched up and we graduated together."

Next, Mrs. Abeson called on Daniel. "Does he live in the house with you?" Daniel asked.

"Oh, yes," said Mrs. Santiago. "He's with me all the time. But he's more than a pet. He's a working dog. And to answer another question I heard before, you should not pat a guide dog when he's working. It can distract him." She leaned down to pat Simba. "But he gets plenty of affection. And if he's not working, and if you ask first, a guide dog's owner might give you permission to pat him."

Mrs. Santiago told them all kinds of interesting

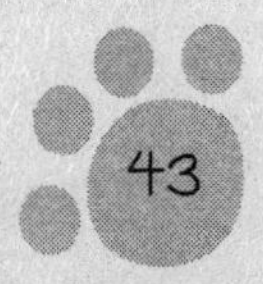

things about working with a guide dog. Like, she said that Simba did not necessarily know which way to go until she told him. So it was up to her to know when to turn right or left. But Simba *did* know how to help her cross a street safely. "If he sees danger, he won't let me cross even if I have given the signal to go," she said.

"What if you want to go to a restaurant?" Caroline asked, without even raising her hand. "Can he go with you?"

Mrs. Santiago nodded. "It's the law. Guide dogs can go anywhere. Simba goes to the post office with me, to stores, to the bank, and to restaurants. He knows how to behave no matter where he is." She smiled down at her dog. "Right, Simba?"

Simba's tail thumped on the floor.

Lizzie loved every minute of Mrs. Santiago's visit. She learned more about guide dogs than she had ever known before, and she even got to try out walking with Simba, holding on to his harness.

At lunchtime, Lizzie asked Maria to sit with her. "Simba is amazing!" she said.

"I know," Maria said. "He makes life so much easier for my mom. He's a real hero."

That was when Lizzie had the best idea ever.

CHAPTER EIGHT

"Shadow could be a guide dog for a blind person!" Lizzie told Charles. They were in Lizzie's room, after school. "I told Maria my idea, and she agrees that he'd be perfect for the job. Think about it!" She reminded Charles of the way Shadow took care of the Bean. "Plus," Lizzie said, "we could be his puppy-raisers. That way we could keep Shadow for a whole year!"

Lizzie explained to Charles what Maria had told her about puppy-raisers and how they were responsible for helping guide dog puppies grow up healthy. They have to teach the puppies about all kinds of places and people so they will be prepared to deal with anything when they are working with a blind person. That means puppy-raisers take their puppies with them to school, to work, to stores, on elevators — everywhere!

Charles had Shadow on his lap. He was stroking the puppy's head. Shadow looked up at him, wrinkling his little forehead as if he were trying hard to understand what Charles and Lizzie were talking about.

Shadow kept hearing his name. He knew the boy and girl were talking about him. They sounded excited. That must mean something good was going to happen!

"Wow," said Charles. He was quiet for a moment. "It sounds like fun. But then — after a year, what happens?"

"Well, then we give him to the training center and they teach him how to be a guide dog, and then he gets matched up with a blind person." Lizzie had talked some more with Maria about how the whole system worked.

"So — after a whole year, we'd have to give him up?" Charles asked. He hugged Shadow, burying his face in the puppy's neck. "I don't know about that."

"It would be hard," Lizzie admitted. When she thought about it, she didn't know how she could do it. If she loved Shadow this much after only a few days, how could she stand letting him go after a year? "Sometimes the puppies don't work out as guide dogs," she said. "If their health isn't perfect or if their personality isn't right. Then the puppy-raisers are allowed to adopt them permanently."

"But Shadow would work out," Charles said.

"Probably," Lizzie said. Then she told Charles about how the puppy-raisers get to go to the graduation, when the blind person and the dog finish training and go off to start their new lives together. "That would be cool," Lizzie added. "Maria says everybody cries."

Charles looked thoughtful. On his lap, Shadow stretched and yawned, waking up from his nap. Then the puppy licked Charles on the chin and

started to squirm around, trying to get off Charles's lap. "Okay, buddy," Charles said. "I'll take him out for a bathroom break," he said to Lizzie.

Lizzie and Charles both knew that a puppy usually needed to go outside right after he woke up. "Great," said Lizzie. "I'm going to go on the Internet and see if I can find out more about how Shadow can become a guide dog."

She turned on her computer. Lizzie loved doing research, especially if it had anything to do with dogs.

It didn't take long for Lizzie to find out that there was a guide dog foundation nearby. It was called Helping Eyes, and it trained ten dogs a year for blind people. Lizzie got more and more excited as she looked at page after page of pictures. Most of the dogs were Labrador retrievers, both black and yellow.

She read about what kind of personality a guide dog should have. There were pictures of the people

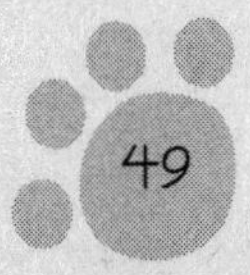

at the foundation testing puppies to see if they had that personality.

She saw pictures of the dogs when they were with their puppy-raisers. They wore little blue vests that read GUIDE DOG IN TRAINING. That way, you could take the puppy into a store or the post office without getting into trouble.

She saw pictures of the same puppies a year or so later. Now they were grown dogs wearing harnesses, being trained to walk a straight line down a sidewalk and to stop at the curb when crossing a street.

And she saw pictures of the dogs at graduation. They looked so proud as they stood beside their new owners.

Lizzie got more and more excited as she read. When Charles came back, she showed him everything she'd found.

"So what do we do next?" Charles asked. "Should we talk to Mom and Dad about it?"

Lizzie shook her head. "Let's wait until we know

if they'll take him," she said. She clicked on a button that read, E-MAIL US!

"Dear Helping Eyes," she wrote. *"My name is Lizzie Peterson. I am ten years old and I have two younger brothers. My family is taking care of a very special black Labrador retriever puppy named Shadow. He is the smartest puppy ever. He's great with people, especially kids. He even kept my littlest brother, Adam, from falling down the stairs! I think he would be a great guide dog for a blind person, and I think our family would make great puppy-raisers."* She asked them to write back right away and let her know if they wanted Shadow to be part of their program.

Maybe, just maybe, Lizzie had found the perfect place for this puppy.

She had a hard time getting to sleep that night. She kept picturing Shadow the puppy in a little blue vest, and Shadow the grown-up dog in a harness, helping a blind person do everything and go everywhere they wanted to go.

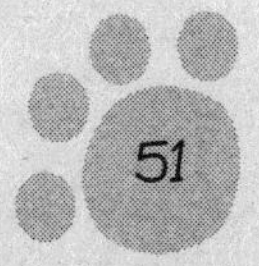

In the morning, Lizzie jumped out of bed and turned on her computer before she even got dressed for school. Maybe the Helping Eyes people had written back!

Sure enough, there was an e-mail waiting for her. *"Re: Shadow,"* the subject line said. Lizzie took a deep breath and clicked to open it.

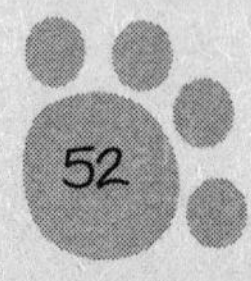

CHAPTER NINE

"Dear Lizzie," the e-mail said. *"Shadow sounds like a wonderful puppy. Unfortunately, we breed almost all of the dogs in our program ourselves."* Lizzie knew what that meant. They kept the best, smartest dogs to be parents to the puppies they trained for blind people. She kept reading. *"Sometimes a breeder will donate a puppy, and if it has papers, is in good health, and has the right personality for being a guide dog, we will accept it. But this is very rare."*

"Lizzie! Breakfast!" Mom called from downstairs.

Lizzie read the rest of the e-mail quickly. *"Thank you for contacting Helping Eyes,"* it said. *"Good luck with Shadow! I'm sure you'll find him a terrific home."* It was signed Nancy Donovan.

Downstairs, Lizzie plopped down in her chair and frowned at her cereal bowl. Shadow trotted over and started to attack her slipper, but not even that could make her smile. Charles gave her a "what happened?" look and she just shook her head. He got the message. The answer was no.

"What's the matter, honey?" Mom asked.

"Nothing," Lizzie said. "Just that we thought maybe we found Shadow a home, but I guess it's not going to work out."

Mom nodded. She could tell Lizzie didn't want to talk about it any more right then. Mom was good about that. "Well, it's good to hear that you're trying," she said. "Because this puppy needs a good home — soon! Our trip is next week."

Charles looked down at the Bean and Shadow, who were rolling around on the floor wrestling. "He looks pretty happy right here," Charles said.

"He does," admitted Mom. "But —"

"We know, we know," Lizzie said. Charles joined

in. "This family is not ready for a full-time dog!" they said together.

On the way to school, Lizzie told Charles what the Helping Eyes people had said.

"But if they could only meet Shadow," Charles said, "they would take him in a minute! He *does* have papers, and he's healthy."

"I know," Lizzie said. "And I think he has the right personality, too. But they're not even interested in meeting him."

"Maybe we could *get* them interested," said Charles.

That got Lizzie thinking. At lunch that day, she told Maria about what Helping Eyes had said. Maria agreed with Charles. "I have a digital camera," she said. "I got it for my birthday, and I already learned to use it. We can take some pictures of Shadow and send them to Helping Eyes. Maybe if they see him, they'll start to understand what a great dog he is."

“That’s an excellent idea!” said Lizzie. “We can explain that he has papers, too. And I was also thinking that we could give him some of the puppy personality tests Helping Eyes uses. I read about them last night. Then they’ll see that he has the perfect personality to be a guide dog.”

Maria came home from school with Lizzie and Charles. Shadow and the Bean met them at the front door. The Bean had peanut butter all over his face, and Shadow was licking him helpfully.

“Oh, what a serious little face!” Maria said when she saw Shadow. “He’s adorable!” She smiled at the Bean. “And you’re pretty cute, too,” she said. “Even with peanut butter all over you.”

The Bean smiled back and woofed at Maria. She laughed. Then she scooped Shadow into her arms. “How about a puppy hug?” she asked. “You know, I never got to spend time with Simba when he was this little, because he was with his puppy-raisers.”

Shadow liked this new girl. Even though she did not have peanut butter on her face, he wanted to lick her on the chin.

They took Shadow outside and played with him for a while. Sammy came over with Rufus and Goldie, and all three dogs tore around the backyard. "Well, that's one of the first tests," Lizzie said, making a note in a little black notebook she was carrying. "Shadow gets along with other dogs."

Maria snapped a few pictures of the dogs playing.

"What other tests are there?" Charles asked.

"I'll explain as we go along," Lizzie told him. "Sammy, why don't you take Rufus and Goldie home so they won't distract Shadow? And Charles, can you go find an umbrella and a tennis ball? Oh, also find an empty soda can, put some coins inside it, and tape it shut." She knew she sounded bossy, but they just didn't have much time.

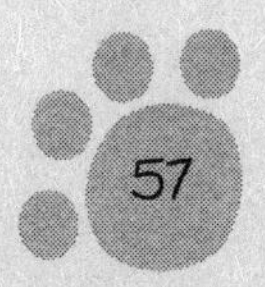

Charles looked curious. "What's all that for?" he asked. It sounded like a scavenger hunt.

"You'll see," Lizzie said. The boys took off and Maria and Lizzie played some more with Shadow.

When Charles and Sammy came back, Lizzie said it was time to start the testing.

"The first test is to see how easily Shadow gets scared by new things," she said. She took the umbrella that Charles had found — it was her old pink Barbie one, from second grade — and called to Shadow. When he trotted over, she snapped the umbrella open, right in his face!

What was that *thing? Shadow thought it was scary, but only at first. He had never seen anything like it! Shadow knew he had to figure it out. He would give it a good sniff.*

Shadow stopped short. He frowned as he tilted his head this way and that, looking at the umbrella. Lizzie put the umbrella on the ground,

upside down. “Come on, Shadow,” she said. She patted the umbrella. The little pup looked at her. Then he looked at the umbrella. Then he walked closer and sniffed it. Then he walked right onto it! Maria snapped a picture of a very serious-looking Shadow sitting inside the pink umbrella.

“Great picture! What a good dog!” Lizzie said, picking Shadow up and giving him a squeeze. “What a brave puppy!” She turned to the others. “Some dogs will run away or bark at the umbrella. But others just want to find out more about it. Curiosity is a good thing for a guide dog to have.”

“Simba’s very curious,” Maria said, nodding. “He’s always sniffing around to make sure things are safe for Mom.”

Lizzie smiled. “Simba would be a great role model for any puppy,” she told her friend. Lizzie felt so lucky. Not only did she have a great new friend — but that friend knew all kinds of things about dogs. Lizzie could tell that she and Maria were going to have some wonderful times together.

Next Lizzie had Charles throw the can full of coins onto the ground behind Shadow. He jumped a little at the sudden rattle, but then he trotted over to sniff at the can and try to figure out why it was so noisy. "Another good sign!" said Lizzie.

After that, Lizzie said it was time to see if Shadow wanted to work with people. Sammy threw the tennis ball across the yard, and Shadow ran after it so fast he tumbled over his own feet. Then he picked it up in his mouth — even though it was almost as big as his head — and trotted back to Lizzie.

That meant he passed the test! Maria got a great picture of that.

Shadow had never had so much fun in his life. These people really knew how to play!

Lizzie wrote everything down in her notebook. "He really does have the perfect personality for a guide dog!" she said. "The tests prove it."

It took her over an hour to type up all the results of their tests. Maria helped her upload the pictures they had taken and choose the best ones. Then, together, they wrote another long e-mail to the people at Helping Eyes. When they said good-bye, both girls held up their hands, fingers crossed. If they were very, very lucky, everything would work out for Shadow — and the Petersons would get to keep him for a whole year!

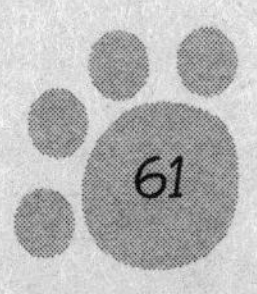

CHAPTER TEN

The subject line said, *"Good news and not-so-good news."* Lizzie felt her heart thumping as she clicked to open the e-mail from Helping Eyes. It had arrived by the time she got home from school.

"Dear Lizzie," it said. *"The good news is that you have convinced us that Shadow would make a good guide dog for a blind person. We will need to examine his papers and do a little more testing, but we would like to gratefully accept your offer to take this dog into our training program."*

Lizzie could hardly believe her eyes! "Charles!" she called. "Come here! Hurry!"

Charles came into her room, carrying Shadow. "What?" he asked. "Did they write back?"

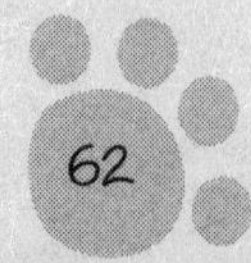

Lizzie read the first part of the e-mail out loud. Reading it again made it seem even more real. When she was done, she and Charles whooped and yelled and gave each other high fives.

Shadow did not know why the children were so happy, but he was happy, too. They stroked him and hugged him and told him what a good puppy he was. He already knew that, but it was always nice to hear.

"So, what's the 'not-so-good' part?" Charles asked. He had seen the subject heading when he leaned over Lizzie's shoulder.

Lizzie scrolled down, and they read together.

"The not-so-good news is this: We require at least one child in our puppy-raiser families to be at least fourteen years old. That means that your family will not be able to raise Shadow — but we hope you'll be part of our program when you are older! Meanwhile, we do have an experienced puppy-raiser

family in your area. The Downeys have agreed to take Shadow. They will contact you today."

Lizzie and Charles looked at each other and then at Shadow, who was still cuddled in Charles's arms. "I can't believe we have to give him up," whispered Lizzie.

When they ran downstairs and told Mom all about it, she reminded them that maybe it was just as well, since they were heading to South Carolina in one week. She also told Lizzie how proud she was. "Imagine, a blind person is going to get a fantastic dog, all because of you. You had a great idea, and you followed through on it, all on your own," she said.

"Well, Charles and Maria and Sammy all helped," Lizzie said modestly. She still wished they could keep Shadow, but Mom was right. It was so cool that he was going where he was needed!

Mom looked down at the Bean, who was crawling through the living room, following Shadow. "I

have a feeling this is going to be very hard on a certain someone," she said, nodding toward the Bean. "He's going to be losing a special friend. Fortunately, he's young enough so that he probably won't be upset for too long. But I'm not sure he could have handled keeping Shadow for a year and *then* giving him up."

Lizzie had to admit that Mom was right. "I'm not sure I could have handled it, either," she said.

The Downeys called that night, after supper. Lizzie talked for a long time with Peter, who was sixteen. He told her all about the two other puppies his family had raised. Lizzie told him all about Shadow and what a special puppy he was. Peter liked hearing about how close Shadow and the Bean had become.

"I bet Shadow will like my little sister, too," he said. "Amanda is crazy about puppies."

Peter told Lizzie that his family had a big, fenced-in yard and that they loved to go for hikes and do other outdoor things. Lizzie had to admit that

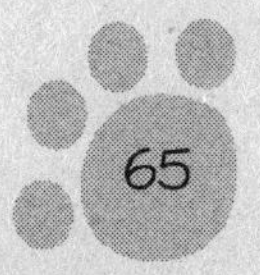

they really might be the perfect family for Shadow.

Afterward, Peter's mom talked to Mrs. Peterson. They agreed that the Downeys would come the next day, Saturday, to meet Shadow.

That night, the Petersons spent a lot of time playing with Shadow and talking about how much they would miss him.

"I feel funny giving Shadow to people we don't even know," said Lizzie. "I mean, I know the Helping Eyes people trust the Downeys . . . but we won't be *sure* they're the right family until we meet them."

"If the Downeys aren't the right family to raise him," Mom said, "we'll just keep looking until we find the perfect family."

Lizzie beamed at her mother.

Mom shrugged. "We only want what's best for Shadow, right?"

Maria came over first thing Saturday morning.

“I can’t stand it!” Lizzie said as they watched Shadow chasing a leaf in the backyard. He tumbled and rolled, making them laugh out loud. “How can I say good-bye to him?”

“But Lizzie,” said Maria. “Just think if Simba never came to my mother. Shadow is going to end up being a guide dog, just like him! Someday he’ll make a real difference in a blind person’s life.”

Lizzie nodded. Maria was right. Lizzie was glad Maria was there. “I know,” she said. “I’m really happy about that. And Peter said we’ll probably be invited to attend when Shadow and his blind handler graduate from the Helping Eyes program next year.” She gave Maria a grateful glance. Lizzie was so happy that she’d finally found a best friend.

Maria was still there when the Downeys arrived in their minivan, complete with a crate in back for Shadow.

Lizzie, Maria, and Charles watched as the

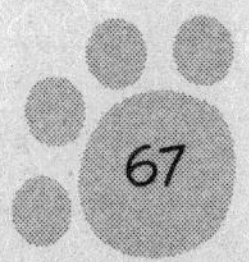

Downeys came up the walk. Lizzie thought they looked like nice people. But were they the right family for Shadow?

"Hey, little dude," Peter said to Shadow when the puppy came running to meet the new people. "What a cutie!"

Lizzie was glad Peter appreciated the puppy. She felt proud of Shadow. "He's so smart, too. I already taught him how to sit before I give him his dinner."

At the word *dinner,* Shadow cocked his head and wrinkled his forehead in that very serious way.

Was it time for food? Yay! Shadow was always ready for a meal. He sat down quickly, looking up at the girl.

Peter laughed. "I see!" he said. He smiled at Lizzie. "You've done a great job with him, I can tell. And you were really smart to figure out that he could be a guide dog."

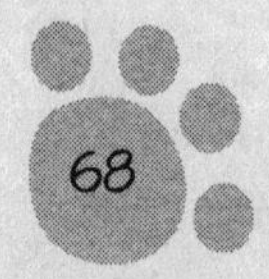

His parents and his little sister laughed, too. Amanda had joined the Bean on the floor next to Shadow, and both of them were patting and hugging him.

Shadow liked these new people. Especially the little one. She smelled delicious!

Lizzie saw that Amanda was gentle with Shadow, just like the Bean was. That was a good sign.

"We brought the Bean a present," said Mrs. Downey. "We thought it might help him not miss Shadow as much." She pulled a stuffed animal out of a shopping bag she had brought in. It was a big, soft, black Lab puppy.

"Uppy!" said the Bean, reaching for it.

Lizzie watched as her little brother hugged the toy close. She had a feeling she might need to hug it herself over the next few days.

Why?

Because now she knew for sure. When the Downeys left, they were going to take Shadow with them. It was obvious that they were the perfect family to raise him.

Lizzie watched Shadow lick Amanda's cheek, and for a second she felt like crying. She had really fallen in love with Shadow, and it was going to hurt to give him up. But Shadow was going to spend a year with this great family, and then he was actually going to learn how to be a guide dog! Giving him up was the right thing to do.

Lizzie looked over at Mom and gave her a special smile and a little nod. *They're the ones,* Lizzie was saying, without using any words.

Mom nodded back. Then she smiled at the Downeys. "How about some lemonade?" she asked.

"Great," said Mr. Downey. "We brought some pictures of the other pups we've raised." They all headed for the kitchen, with Shadow trotting along after Amanda. Lizzie could tell that the Downeys would take great care of him.

It wasn't easy giving up Shadow. But Lizzie knew it was the right thing to do. And she knew that there would probably be another puppy coming along sometime soon, a puppy who needed her family's help finding just the right place to live. Lizzie couldn't wait to meet it!

PUPPY TIPS

Some puppies, like Shadow, learn very fast. Other puppies take longer to figure things out, but stick with it! With time and patience, you can teach your puppy good manners and more.

There are lots of books about how to train your puppy, or you can do some research on the Internet. You might also be able to find dog training classes in your neighborhood.

Always be kind to your puppy when you are training it. Use lots of praise, pats, and treats. If your dog would rather play with a ball than eat a biscuit, use playtime as a reward instead of food.

Don't yell or jerk the leash. And remember that most puppies can't pay attention for much more than ten minutes at a time. Keep your training sessions short!

Dear Reader,

A few years ago my niece Katie was the puppy raiser for a yellow Lab puppy. She was named Oreo. Katie took care of Oreo for a whole year, and Oreo went everywhere with her, dressed in a little blue vest that said, "Guide Dog in Training." After a year, Oreo went off for more training. Katie got to go to her graduation.

Katie said that raising Oreo was lots of fun but also a big responsibility. It made Katie sad to give her up, but it makes her feel good to know that Oreo is helping to make someone's life better every day.

Yours from the Puppy Place,
Ellen Miles

P.S. For another extremely helpful pup, check out HONEY.

DON'T MISS THE NEXT
PUPPY PLACE ADVENTURE!

Here's a peek at RASCAL!

"That's Susan, from work," Mrs. Peterson said. "Susan?" she asked the woman. "What are you —"

"I can't take it anymore," said the woman. "We tried. We really did. But we just can't deal with this dog." She had to shout to be heard over the puppy's barking.

At the same time, a baby in a car seat inside the car started to wail, and the two blond little kids strapped in next to him began to yell, "Mommy, Mommy, Mommy!"

Lizzie walked over to the woman and took the leash from her hand. "Come on, pup," she said, leaning down to scoop the excited puppy into her arms. "Quiet down. *Shh, shh,* you're being silly."

Let me down! Let me down! Let me down! The puppy wriggled and barked. What good was being in a new place if you couldn't explore? Oh, well, if he couldn't get down, maybe he could at least make a new friend!

The puppy struggled a little, but then seemed to decide that he liked being in Lizzie's arms. He gave a few last barks before he started to lick her face instead. Starting at her chin, he worked his way up to the inside of her nostrils, which made Lizzie giggle because it tickled so much. She couldn't believe how friendly the little guy was.

After a grateful smile at Lizzie, the woman had turned back to the car to talk to her children. "It's okay, guys," she said. "These people will take good care of Rascal." She unbuckled the kids' seat belts so they could climb out of the car, and took the baby out of his car seat, settling him on her hip.

"Rascal!" Lizzie loved that name. It was perfect for the wild little puppy.

Mom came over to give the woman a hug. "Susan works with me at the paper," she explained to the rest of the family. "She's a proofreader there. She catches all the mistakes in the articles I write."

By then, Charles had joined Lizzie. He was stroking Rascal's wiry coat. "What kind of dog is Rascal?" he asked.

"He's a Jack Russell terrier," said Lizzie and Susan at the same time.

Lizzie had recognized Rascal's breed the moment she saw him. He looked just like the Jack Russell on her "Dog Breeds of the World" poster: small and muscular, with a short, stubby tail. His ears stood up halfway and then flopped over, and he had a sharp, pointy black nose and bright, shiny black eyes. He was curious and ready for action!

Susan nodded at Lizzie. "So you've heard of this breed. I never had, until my kids saw one in the movies. Once they saw that dog, they bugged me and bugged me and bugged me to get a Jack Russell terrier. They thought it was the cutest dog they ever saw."

"Jack Russells are definitely adorable," Lizzie agreed.

ABOUT THE AUTHOR

Ellen Miles likes to write about the different personalities of dogs. She is the author of more than 28 books, including the Puppy Place and Taylor-Made Tales series as well as The Pied Piper and other Scholastic Classics. Ellen loves to be outdoors every day, walking, biking, skiing, or swimming, depending on the season. She also loves to read, cook, explore her beautiful state, and hang out with friends and family. She lives in Vermont.

If you love animals, be sure to read all the adorable stories in the Puppy Place series!